MASTER OF THE FUNNY VERSE
Volume I

By Wallerton Keys

<u>**Dedication:**</u>

If I were possessed of a little more of the above quality then this book wouldn't have taken so long to manifest as a tangible thing.

Introduction:

It has long been said that laughter is the best medicine. I believe such to be true. But, tell this to a man who is suffering from malaria and he is likely to call you a liar. His preference would be quinine and there is a good chance that it might be the better medicine of the two. So, in rare cases, I will admit that laughter is not the best medicine. It very much depends on what ails you. I, personally, am not medically trained in any way and yet I feel qualified in attempting to deliver the medicine that is laughter. My medium is comedic verse and it is administered through the written word. Should you read any one of the enclosed works and not feel immediately better then I consider that I have failed and that you may indeed require conventional medical treatment.

Table of Contents

Guide to "Watson a Name"

Master the Funny Verse

This master of the funny verse
Is subject to a witch's curse
She placed on him in days of yore,
A distant 1564…

"From now until the end of time
Your words must be the perfect rhyme
And humour must be present too -
If not, then comes an end for you!"

So many lives from birth to hearse,
He moved through time with rhyming verse,
All written in comedic vein
To best amuse and entertain.

Success and fame meant longer life
But often came the critic's knife,
For just one single bad review
Saw malady and death ensue.

So, laugh please if you wouldn't mind
Or smile if you feel inclined,
Pray too, appreciate the wit,
Alas, my life depends on it.

Although I feel I must confess,
It could've been my fault, I guess?
Perhaps it was a little harsh to dunk her in that lake…
Then burn her at the stake.

David

There once was a barman called David
Whose cocktails were expertly flavoured
Regrettably though
To his unending woe
They were guzzled instead of being savoured

Steve

There was a magician called Steve
Who could do things you wouldn't believe
But he hasn't been seen
Since December thirteen
When he disappeared up his own sleeve

Said a Curious Child

A curious child stopped a teacher one day
And said, "Miss, I have something important to
say…
I've been learning to read and to write and to
spell
But sometimes it hasn't been going so well
And it's starting to make me a little upset,
There are quite a few things that I REALLY
don't get!

"How did *think* become *thought*?
How did *bring* become *brought*?
Who said *teach* should be *taught*?
And that *buy* should be *bought*?
How did *seek* become *sought*?
How did *catch* become *caught*?
Who said *fight* should be *fought*?
I think somebody ought
To make *bring* become *brung*
And *think* become *thunk*
Because *sing* becomes *sung*
And *drink* becomes *drunk.*
And if *break* becomes *broke*
And *wake* becomes *woke*

It's totally fine then if *speak* becomes *spoke*,
But then *make* becomes *made*, yes it does I'm afraid,
So why doesn't *take* become *toke* then,
Or *tade*?
In fact, *take* becomes *took*
And then *shake* becomes *shook*
But then *bake* isn't *book*
Because *book* has been taken
And somewhere in here,
the word *shake* becomes *shaken*
But *break* isn't *breaken*, it's *broken*
And *speak* becomes *spoken*
And *wake* becomes *woken*
But *bake* isn't *boken*,
It's *BAKED*!

It's a terrible shame
When words look just the same
But don't sound just the same
Or they sound just the same
But don't look just the same
And I'd so like the name
Of the person to blame.

I see *laughter* and *daughter*

Then *after* and *water*
(Two longer, two shorter)
Then *quarter* and *slaughter.*
There's *weight* and there's *great.*
There's *fate* and then *bait*
But I hate the word *height* since it looks just like *weight*
And this happens despite
The words *quite, sight, invite, fight, delight* and *tonight.*
And this would be all right
Except now I've turned eight
I am sure number eight sounds like *weight* and not *height*!

We've got *puff* and there's *stuff.*
We've got *rough* and there's *tough.*
But then *though* doesn't go
And *through* simply won't do,
As for *trough*, it's just off.
And who put the "w" in number two
When it should've begun number one?

And though *three* is just fine,
Number four looks like *our*
Then you put in an "l" and it turns into *flour.*

But what of the flower that grows in the garden?
You take off the "f" and I'm begging your pardon,
It's *lower*, then *slower* and *blower* and *mower*,
But look here comes *power* and *tower* and *shower*.

Then if *blow* becomes *blew*
And *grow* becomes *grew*,
Shouldn't *show* become *shew*?
Shouldn't *glow* become *glew*?
And if *fly* becomes *flew*
Shouldn't *try* become *trew*?
No, it's *tried* and I've cried trying to work it all out,
And by the way…
How did that "b" get in *doubt*?

And if *said* sounds like *shed* but is spelt just like *paid*
And if *read* can be *read* and no changes are made
Then *breed* becomes *bred* and *lead* becomes *led*
And *flee* becomes *fled*
But *agree*'s not *agred*

Although *feed* becomes *fed*
But does *free* become *Fred*?
No, it's *freed*
And then *need* isn't *Ned*,
No, it's *needed* instead!

Well, the teacher replied,
Though she thought for a while
And running away simply wasn't her style.
This teacher, the first one in history we think,
(Who started when desks still had vials of ink)
Took a very deep breath and announced with some woe,
"My dear, to be honest, I really don't know."

<u>Benny</u>
There once was a miser called Benny
Whose spending was little if any
And his laziness too
Made it fittingly due
He died busily spending a penny

Melancholy Wally

A very melancholy fellow didn't know the sun was yellow
For his eyes so very rarely left the ground.
He'd often sit and play the cello, would this melancholy fellow,
Something sad and rather mellow was the sound.
And though the neighbours they would bellow at this melancholy fellow
He would finish off the tune that he'd begun.
Then, while reading from Othello, he'd eat chocolate and marshmallow
Because this, you see, was his idea of fun.

Now, although his name was Wallace, all who knew him called him Wally,
So as Melancholy Wally he was known.
And when Melancholy Wally took a walk, he took his collie
For he hated going walking on his own.
And he would always hold a brolly since he knew it to be folly
To expect it wouldn't rain while they're outside.

And if a passer-by said, "Golly! You're a little off your trolley.",
He would take this sort of comment in his stride.

Not far away lived Gloomy Glenda, she was tall and rather slender
But would spend a lot of time just feeling blue.
She'd pretend that her agenda was a blend of her attending trendy parties or a secret rendezvous.
And if you wanted to befriend a girl like Glenda or extend a hand of friendship
She'd be sure to turn you down.
Because a broken heart does render Glenda number one contender
For the most unhappy person in the town.

But on this day, the sky was grey, the month of May was underway
And Gloomy Glenda had come out to get the mail.
A gust of wind though blew the door and Gloomy Glenda loudly swore
Because it locked and then the clouds began to hail.

Alas, the hail began to pelt her so she looked
around for shelter
Then quite suddenly she felt a man behind.
Above her head was an umbrella from a
melancholy fella
Who was well equipped for happ'nings of this
kind.
And it was love at second sight because at first
they got a fright
But as they stood and looked each other in the
eyes,
The pair of them began to smile which hadn't
happened in a while
But was something neither one could well
disguise.

Subsequent to having met, she learned to play
the clarinet,
They formed a musical quartet with two new
friends.
The melancholy fell away as did the
gloominess that day
And life together, they are hoping, never ends.

The Honest Member

Mister Speaker, Mister Speaker,
Though my argument grows weaker,
I'll continue – I'm afraid you have no choice.
Any heckling I'll ignore,
Since I've heard it all before.
What I care for is the sound of my own voice.

Mister Speaker, Mister Speaker,
I'm a champion critiquer
Who has mastered the belittling point of view.
No man or subject matter's safe
From my uncompromising strafe
And I'm most righteous when I'm guilty of it
too.

Mister Speaker, Mister Speaker,
I'm no blatent havoc wreaker,
I prefer to wreak my havoc on the sly.
With deception and distraction
And my innocent reaction,
We've the glory of the rumour and the lie.

Mister Speaker, Mister Speaker,
Though I'm no attention seeker,

I will give reporters something they can use.
And I don't mind being quoted wrongly
Since I never feel that strongly,
Just as long as Mummy sees me on the news.

Mister Speaker, Mister Speaker,
I'm no information leaker
As it's quite against my principles of course.
But money large and well disguised
Could see my principles revised,
Without the prick of any conscience or
remorse.

Mister Speaker, Mister Speaker,
Now the situation's bleaker
Since we duly dilly-dally as we do.
Indecision, imprecision,
Disagreement and derision
Is no recipe for pushing something through.

Mister Speaker, Mister Speaker,
Is there anyone who's meeker
Or as privileged as I have been from birth?
With the good amongst us lost,
Disillusioned, double-crossed,
It would appear we have inherited the earth.

Mrs. McKenzie Shops for Shoes

Mrs. McKenzie stood in the frenzy looking for something nice,
Because Mrs. McPhail was having a sale with all of her shoes at half-price.
Mrs. McLeod was there in the crowd and keen to get something in blue,
But Mrs. McBeth was frightened to death and didn't know what to do.
Mrs. McCready had been a bit greedy and purchased too many to carry,
While young Miss McKnight sought something in white, to wear on the day she would marry.
Mrs. McDowell had appealed for a foul because someone had elbowed her nose,
While Mrs. McGill was threatening to kill the lady who'd trod on her toes.
Mrs. McCoy was jumping for joy as she'd just found the shoes of her dreams,
But Mrs. McNaught was rather distraught and coming apart at the seams.
Mrs. McPhee had tried twenty-three, but couldn't find any that fitted,
Though Mrs. McNair found a casual pair, to go with some socks she had knitted.

Mrs. McDougall, terribly frugal, had left because "nothing was cheap",
But Mrs. McRae found some heels that were grey and so perfect she started to weep.
Mr. McBride, who was waiting outside, had completely lost sight of his wife,
While Mrs. McCall had taken a fall, and frankly she feared for her life.
Mrs. McMaster had tried to move faster but lost in the race for a pair
To Mrs. McVicar, who'd moved a lot quicker and held the shoes punching the air.
Now Mrs. McPhail, to little avail, had tried to calm everyone down
And Mrs. McPherson, the chief sales-person, was anxious and wearing a frown,
Until Mr. McCann, the security man, saw a car with a chauffeur outside,
Then in walked the Queen seeking something in green as the rest of them stood goggle-eyed!

Avuncular Verse

My Uncle Bernard is so learned,
He knows all there is to know.
He knows everything up high
And he knows everything down low.
He knows all the answers left
And he knows all the answers right.
He knows all about the day
And he knows all about the night.

My Uncle Bart is just as smart,
A live encyclopedia
Who gobbles information up
For no-one's mind is greedier.
And if you thought your reading fast
He'd read a book much speedier,
And if you thought you read a lot,
Well, he is so much read-ier.

And when they got together,
Would they talk about the weather?
No, that didn't happen ever,
Each would try to be more clever
Than the other one of course.
And often they'd start shouting

Till their voices would be hoarse.
And sometimes it got violent
Or they'd sulk and both go silent,
But mostly they would argue
On a subject never heard of
And babble lengthy sentences
That no-one knew a word of,
Or debating technicalities
That really didn't matter,
Like whether rain on roofs
Would either pitter or would patter.
But neither of them ever
Would admit the other right,
Regardless of how ludicrous
The argument or fight.

Eventually it dawned on me
These men were not so bright,
Their contribution to the world
Being only very slight.

They never helped a neighbour out
Or cheered a crying child,
Encouraged someone's artistry
Or simply looked and smiled.

Too little observation
Of what actually occurred
And too much concentration
On a version they preferred.

No questioning or thought
About the knowledge they possessed,
No eagerness to verify
Or put it to the test.

So were they really thinking men
With intellect to burn?
Or just a sponge for data
And unable to discern?

Quite recently they left us,
Moving on to pastures new
And I'd like to say they're sorely missed
But this might not be true.

<u>Walt's in a Flat</u>

Walt's in a flat
Where he lives all alone,
Apart from a kitten
Whose name is unknown
And a goldfish called Gary
Who thinks he's a shark
And a dog who's called
Johann Sebastian Bark.

Walt plays his piano,
Some Ludwig or Fred.
He'll practice and drill
Till his fingers turn red,
Then he's out for a walk
On a much-needed break
To a park near his flat
With some trees and a lake.

He walks past a girl
Who's been stung by a bee,
She has gasped and proceeded
To scream at High C.
"Impressive," thinks Walt,
"That's impressive indeed.

For any soprano
Who's ever High C'ed
Would be proud of the purity
And the sustain
That she rather unwittingly
Strove to attain."

Then he strolls past a mynah bird
Up in a tree
Who was squawking a Major third
Slightly off-key.

Past a swan
Who vibrated her bill
And created a delicate trill
Then looked over at Walt
Who acknowledged her skill.

Past a crow
Whose divertimento
Was as good as the frog and the duck
Who were trying their luck
At the "Flower Duet" by Delibes
To applause of a kind
From a Great Crested Grebe.
Of course, Walt was applauding it too,

But while doing so knew
That his walk had to end undelayed
For his fingers were back to their usual shade…
A piano sits idle and needs to be played!

So, Walt turned on his heels
And went back,
Past a cyclist stood cursing a tack -
Something sharp had created a flat,
"Well, there's nothing more natural than that,"
Said Walt.

Upon his return,
He opened his door,
The kitten is meowing
And hard to ignore.
Walt gave it some food
And is playing an étude
When a thought comes to mind
Of the nominal kind…

At the risk of being bitten
He picked up the kitten
And said,
"I'm going to call you Pianoforté!"
And he ruffled the fur on its head

"The reasoning is that your fur is so soft
But you're loud when you wish to be fed.
I may sometimes resort
To Piano for short
But your name is Pianoforté."
Then Walt laughed, sat back down
And continued to play.

Not too much later,
A knock at the door.
Walt's neighbour beside him
Had done this before,
"You're persona non grata
I'm midst a sonata,"
Yelled Walt and continued to play.
There were several more knocks,
Maybe shouting as well
But eventually he went away.

Now the sun never sets
Upon Walt and his pets
For they live in a world of their own,
And when Walt's in a flat
Playing a waltz in A flat
There is harmony, tempo and tone.

Two Haiku

That is so like you
Meeting a man called Mike who
Dares to rhyme haiku

I had a shower
And smelled just like a flower
For about an hour

Ken

There once was a farmer called Ken
Who owned a peculiar hen
For the eggs she would lay
Contained raspberry souffle´
But it only occurred now and then

Bruce

There once was a convict called Bruce
Who was two weeks away from the noose
But a beard that was fake
And a file in a cake
Were proven of very great use

This is Getting Old

He lost his vim and his vigour,
She lost her looks and her figure.
He found his hair getting thinner,
She found that grey was the winner.

She hated losing at Bingo,
He hated young people's lingo.
She loved her comfortable slippers,
He loved his toe-nail clippers.

She lost their pensioner passes,
He lost his keys and his glasses.
She found her skin getting wrinkled,
He found it slow when he tinkled.

He missed his hands never shaking,
She missed her knees never aching.
He hit his head and was cursing,
She hit their shed while reversing.

They felt the cold more than ever,
They sold their house which was clever.
They moved to much warmer weather
And just grew older together.

<u>Jack the Vicar</u>

Poor old Jack the country vicar
Had more recently looked sicker
With his waistline getting thicker
And a very dodgy ticker
That would tend to beat much quicker
If he drank a lot of liquor
Or whenever he would bicker
With his curate, Mr Dicker,
A notorious nit-picker
With a fishy bumper-sticker
Who would criticise and snicker
Since his arguments were slicker.

Soon a candle it will flicker
Leading to a bucket-kicker
In the shape of Jack the vicar
So... Amen.

From a Hilltop

Never mind the light of the moon
Shining down 'pon Brigadoon,
Compared to thee its effort fails,
A brave attempt at beauty pales.

And never mind the city lights,
More dazzling than the poet writes,
Defeated as they try to be
The thing that is attracting me.

And never mind the air I breathe,
I'm more than happy to bequeath.
Alone up here alone with you,
More striking than the artist drew,
Forgive me if I lose control,
My saucy, brand new blow-up doll.

Tony

There once was a father called Tony
Who bought his young daughter a pony
But it got all too much
For the upkeep was such
That his level of broke became stony

Cat Calling

An artistic pedigree Persian tom
With a fair degree of pride,
Sits back in admiration,
Pug-face tilted to one side.

A work of ragged beauty
From a radical idea,
Original and challenging
With geometric flair.

But meanwhile just behind the cat,
A pair of newlyweds,
The wife is standing mortified,
The husband's pallor spreads.
Alas, his little feline friend
Had torn her couch to shreds.

Charlie

There once was a biker called Charlie
Who ate meat and rode on a Harley
Then he married a vegan
A nice girl called Megan
And now he eats kale and barley

Anecdate

The fish was fat sodden, the chips overdone,
The flattest of fizzy, the stalest of bun,
I partook as a last-ditch attempt to have fun
But this date was at best an unfortunate one.

He enquired, "Is everything going okay?"
I nodded and smiled which didn't betray
My desperately trying to think of a way
To escape without causing him too much
dismay.

Of all the excuses I'd used in the past
Not one of them suited the problem here cast,
I needed a good one and needed it fast
But my courteous pretence, it just didn't last.
I stood up and ran leaving patrons aghast
And my previous record for shame was
surpassed.

The Meanderthals

Here come the Meanderthals
Slowly down the street,
They're looking for the shopping malls
And sweating from the heat.

Here come the Meanderthals,
They left their own backyard,
Now throwing down some gutter balls
Of cultural regard.

Here come the Meanderthals,
Loudly they will speak,
And bouncing off the ancient walls
An asinine critique.

Here come the Meanderthals,
So very hard to miss.
Nothing untoward befalls
Their unenlightened bliss.

Caravan Dan

Caravan Dan is a caravan man,
He's been that way since his life began.
His own caravan is spick and span
And he's possibly the world's greatest caravan fan.

He gets inspiration from his Caravan Gran,
From his Uncle Stan and his Auntie Jan.
They meet and have a chat whenever they can,
Together they're a serious caravan clan.

Now, Caravan Dan is a family man
With a wife called Fran and a daughter, Roxanne.
He tows his caravan behind a blue sedan,
Following his caravan master plan.

They've been to South Sudan, they've been to North Milan,
They've been to West Japan and to the Isle of Man
Because Dan knows of nothing else better than…
Travelling the world in a caravan.

Their breakfast each morning is raisin bran
And Fran's not bad with a frying pan.
The girls' favourite treat is a pecan flan,
But Dan's always been a chocolate brownie man.

But then one day in East Bhutan,
They heard from the local anchor man
About a law for a world-wide caravan ban
And they only had a month before the ban began.

Well, Caravan Dan was a broken man,
So were Gran, Uncle Stan and Auntie Jan,
But Fran, Dan's patient and loving spouse
Was secretly glad they'd have to live in a house!

Phil

An old street performer called Phil
Made his money by standing quite still
Though he did catch the eye
Of the odd passer-by
He more frequently just caught a chill

Frankenstein

Hats off to Dr Frankenstein,
He pieced together something fine:
A monster made of men deceased,
A hideous, ungainly beast
Who terrorised the neighbourhood
As any decent monster should.
While all he sought was charity,
He found, at best, barbarity.
So, turned on who created him
And things became a little grim.
Alas, poor Dr Frankenstein
Quite ignorantly crossed a line -
Don't tug on Mother Nature's gown
Or consequence will track you down.

Larry

There once was a bachelor called Larry
Who, at last, met the girl he would marry
But a wedding night fright
Was a touch more than slight
For it turned out her real name was Barry

<u>Helping Bradley</u>

Don't be so negative, Bradley!
All your *no's* and your *not's* and your *never's.*
If it were I, I'd be eager to try
One of many potential endeavours.

The bright side's the right side, young Bradley,
When you're seeking encouraging signs.
If you dwell on the smell of defeat
You'll repeat a past failing and all its confines.

And don't be so anti advice you receive,
That is not how your battles are won.
It was just my intention to help you, my boy,
And it looks like my work here is done.

For I see that a light has come on in your eyes,
I can see your demeanour has changed.
Well, of course you can ask me a question my
boy…
No, I'd not like my face re-arranged.

A Piece of Information

Let me introduce you to a piece of information
That may help you in your life if you possess
the inclination
To expand your many horizons and improve
your situation,
So prepare to reap the benefits of your
imminent education.
But before I can divulge this vital piece of
information,
I must have from you a genuine and solemn
declaration
As a promise that it won't be used to gain some
domination
Over others far less fortunate who lack the
aspiration
And are yet to take receipt of this important
assertation.
Now, of course I wouldn't want to cause you
any aggravation
But I feel that this is more than necessary
trepidation
Since the learning of this data will be such a
revelation

That you may be forced to leave us all and take
a short vacation
To allow yourself the time to give the fullest
contemplation
To the datum I'm about to share with no
exaggeration.
And it's not that there's a desperate need for
over-complication
But I very strongly recommend some careful
concentration
Should you truly wish to comprehend its every
connotation
And attach to it your very own precise
interpretation
Then, of course, it would be incorrect to speed
dissemination
Or neglect my duly offering the needed
preparation
To deliver this remarkable, profound
communication.
Now, I'm nearly at the end of this, my formal
presentation
And I thank you for your patience and your
kind consideration
Please be careful not to taint it with a snap
adjudication.

Finally, here it is presented now, enough procrastination,
"The greater the build-up, the greater the potential for disappointment."

Jude
There once was a blacksmith called Jude
Who was surly, uncultured and rude
And a little bit dull
From a kick to the skull
For a horse must be carefully shoed

Ricky
There was a detective called Ricky
Who once solved a case that was tricky
The abduction of Michael
While riding his cycle
Was just someone taking the Mickey

<u>Mr. Bottletop</u>

Mr. Bottletop talks to the trees and the birds.
He stands in the forest and utters these words,
"Trees, you have branches. Birds, you have
wings.
How did you come to grow such useful things?
Birds, you have feathers. Trees, you have
leaves.
All that I have is these arms in my sleeves.
But they don't make me fly when I flap them
about
And my arms don't grow leaves when I stand
with them out."
Then Mr. Bottletop breathes out a sigh
And says "Bumpledump-dink! If I only knew
why."

Mr. Bottletop sings to the flowers and bees
But before he begins, he goes down on his
knees.
He sings, "Flowers, you have petals. Bees, you
have wings.
How did you come to grow such useful things?
Bees, you have honey. Flowers smell sweet.
All that I have is two legs and two feet.

But my legs cannot run me as fast as a bee
And my feet have a smell that embarrasses
me."
Then Mr. Bottletop closes one eye
And says "Bumpledump-dink! If I only knew
why."

When Mr. Bottletop's day is near done,
He sits by the window and watches the sun.
He says "Sun, once again I must bid you
goodbye
But the moon and the stars will soon light up
the sky.
Where is it you go at the end of each day?
Wherever it is, it looks too far away.
I imagine it's splendid but quite hard to find
When all that I have is two eyes and a mind."
And while Mr. Bottletop's wondering where,
The shadows grow longer and then disappear.
Mr. Bottletop frowns and sits back in his chair
And says "Bumpledump-dink! Life is truly
unfair."

In The Garden

Basil and Rosemary sit in the garden,
The time is most quietly spent.
An hour might pass in the blink of an eye
And neither would know where it went.

A twitter of sparrows, a rustle of leaves,
But seldom the silence disturbs
And never between them is any word spoken
For Basil and Rosemary are herbs.

Terence

There was a teenager called Terence
Who really did not like his parents
If they tried to be nice
Or impart some advice
They were met with complete incoherence

Ted

There was an inventor called Ted
Who spent most of his time in a shed
For his life's work had been
To create a machine
That removed all the gluten from bread

Watson a Name

A man called Felix Horstid ran a marathon today,
While Andy Zoff was very quick and probably first away.

Anita Finnish decorates and uses masking tape,
While Owen Munny ran up debts from which he can't escape.

Paige Turner is a novelist who's having much success.
Faye Clegg, a recent amputee, conceals it with a dress.

Chris Plettis and Stu Dapple run a popular food truck.
Neil E. Haddim likes to fish but doesn't have much luck.

Kaye Ottick causes trouble and confusion all the time.
Eve Ninall and Polly Stogg are always fighting crime.

The cause of the disaster was a man called Hugh Manerra.
George Ropping stood in disbelief as witness to the terror.

Ben Schwarma is a substitute who never gets to play.
Bo Nydle loves the sofa and it's where he's been all day.

Herbie Vore eats vegetables but will not touch a steak.
Stan Duppallday has achy feet and really needs a break.

Prue Freeding knows her grammar and her punctuation too.
Bill Jarrone is in his shed with handsaw, wood and glue.

Cara Lahm's too sensitive and always going off.
Saul Bettanow is back at work recovered from his cough.

Barb Dwyer married Barry Kade to make a perfect pair.
Hugh Jonner is about to be inducted as the mayor.

Ewan Hoozarmee challenged the man who threatened to knock him flat.
Sonia Head is not too bright and looking for her hat.

Rufus Leeking looks outside and hopes the rain will cease.
Marion Cupples loves the line "…forever hold your peace."

Anne Teeks enjoys collectibles and sells them at her stall.
Sue Tavama spends her days just standing in the hall.

Trudy Light received good news and now she's on cloud nine.
Freida Livery likes a deal when ordering online.

Annie Norma Sproffit has a business that's expanding.
E. Victor Tennant is a landlord who shows little understanding.

Doug Deep was under pressure but he rallied and prevailed.
Petra Fyde was frozen with her face entirely paled.

Benny Fishal looks as though he'd do us all some good.
Rhys Ponsible is very good at doing what he should.

Sergeant Laura Byding keeps the criminals at bay,
She catches thieves like Nick McCarr and has them put away.

The safety gear is all in place for Justin Casey Falls.
Lou Swire's always puzzled when his car completely stalls.

Rory Motion likes to wear his heart upon his sleeve,
While Edna Randz had more bad luck than she could quite believe.

Amos Keeto buzzed around annoying everyone.
I. Malooney took too long to find the final pun.

Hugh
There once was a rich kid called Hugh
Who had so very little to do
That he strayed into drugs
And colluding with thugs
Now his room's rather lacking a view

Tina
There once was a gardener called Tina
Whose fingers could not have been greener
But she planted her feet
And grew wispy like wheat
Which did radically change her demeanour

<u>**Romance**</u>

She was a beautiful, dutiful,
Beauty full of grace,
With a wilful, thrillful
Smile on her face.
And she was youthful, truthful,
Delicate as lace,
With a thoughtful, distortful
Head in outer space.

He was a tasteful, wasteful,
Playboy full of charm,
With a resourceful, forceful
Power to disarm.
He was deceitful, cheatful,
Bereft of any qualm
And was regretful, forgetful
Of causing any harm.

It was a blissful, kissful
Day on which they met.
They wrote a zestful, jestful,
Fleeting novelette,
Turned into hopeless, copeless,
Motionless regret.

But then a tearless, fearless
Departure under threat.

She ended up an aimless, blameless
Girl without a plan.

He ended up a wifeless, lifeless,
Truthless, toothless very, very
Bitter old man.

Natalie
There once was a pauper called Natalie
Who tended to dress rather tattily
Then she found a rare stamp
Had a lifestyle revamp
Now her interests are clothes and philately

Prue
An expectant young mother called Prue
Whose baby was well overdue
When the time did arrive
There were actually five
Who'd been actively forming a queue

Mr. Wichita Carruthers

Mr. Wichita Carruthers had a sister and two brothers
And he really rather missed her when she went away to sea.
But as for his two brothers, Mr. Wichita Carruthers,
Truly wished they'd different mothers
But he knew that couldn't be.
He was stuck with these two brothers, Mr. Wichita Carruthers,
They would trick him, they would trap him,
They would tie him to a tree.
And Mr. Wichita Carruthers used to claim they were another's brothers –
"Damn it!" he would often say, "These two are not with me!"
He grew so tired of his two brothers, Mr. Wichita Carruthers,
And complained of them to others over endless cups of tea.
"Mr. Wichita Carruthers," said the others of his brothers,
"These gentlemen are mental men; in jail they should be."

Mr. Wichita Carruthers found it hard to disagree.

But then, the sister came back home – a leave-of-absentee,
And saw that little much had changed between her brothers three.
"Why can't you leave poor Wichita alone and let him be?" said she.
But when the two Carruthers brothers heard this earnest plea,
They turned upon their sister, in their eyes a crazy glee.
Alas, they didn't know that while she'd been away, Marie,
Had learnt to fight and kick and strike to masterful degree.
And what befell was close to hell, a devastating spree -
The brothers two lay staring through the stars that they could see.
While Wichita was watching on and whispering, "Whoopee!"
He felt a little sad for them… but only fleetingly.

O'Blivious

Mr O'Reilly would disappear slyly whenever it came to his round,
And Mr O'Malley had such a beer belly that parts of him couldn't be found.
All the O'Flanagans' evening shenanigans only occurred when they drank,
While Mr O'Hare had eased his despair and for this, he had whisky to thank.
Mr O'Shea, in his usual way, got pie-eyed and tried picking a fight,
While Mr O'Kane simply couldn't refrain from a drink or three every night.
Mr O'Flynn lived on tonic and gin, he was terribly thin and was shrinking,
And Mr O'Donahue's marriage had gone askew probably due to his drinking.
Mr O'Neill had imbibed a great deal and then thrown up all over the floor,
And Mr O'Connor would soon be a goner – his liver could take little more.
Mr O'Grady, who'd cornered a lady, was sloshed and attempting sincere,
While Mr O'Rourke was being kind of a dork after drinking a skinful of beer.

Mr O'Doyle did so like to spoil the mood with a boozy tirade,
And Mr O'Hearn seemed unable to learn that his problems weren't gone, just delayed.
Mr O'Keefe was of the belief that vodka would cure his gout,
And Mr O'Dowd felt especially proud for he'd drowned all his sorrows with stout.
Mr O'Leary would always get teary and reminisce when he was drunk,
But Mr O'Toole had collapsed in a pool of a liquid that steamed and stunk.
It was rowdy, unruly, unpleasant and duly, the bar staff conceded defeat,
So, Mr O'Brien, who ran the Red Lion, chucked everyone out in the street.

<u>Frank</u>
There once was a lawyer called Frank
Whose ethical sense really stank
He'd win every case
For the guiltiest face
And then laugh all the way to the bank

<u>Nun the Wiser</u>

Sister Mary Cavalcade
Loved tea and toast with marmalade.
Her habit was to rise at dawn
And don a habit crisply worn.
She also loved the morning dew,
The flowers opening up anew,
She loved the birds and loved the bees
But not in combination please.

And Sister Mary Cavalcade
Got down upon her knees and prayed
For courage, strength and moral good
For those who might and those who should.
She prayed for other souls as well,
The legion sinners bound for Hell
And even one for self, since yes,
Those hips could ache a little less.

Sister Mary Cavalcade,
Whose skin has dried, whose hair has greyed,
Conventional she's always been
From early 1917.
She wonders where the decades went
And stirs a bit of discontent,

Then sneaks a sip from silver flask,
From whence it came, you needn't ask.

And Sister Mary Cavalcade,
On temper fell a darker shade,
When sat inside the inglenook
And having closed her favourite book.
She clearly had seen better days,
Downcast, she quite forlornly says,
"You've long been my advisor…
But I fear I'm none the wiser."

Fred

There once was a signalman, Fred
Who spent too much time in his bed
And his favourite joke
For his wife, when he woke…
"I'm a railway sleeper," he said

Pierre

There once was a chef called Pierre
Who lived way up high in the air
On the forty-first floor
He enjoyed even more
A slightly chilled chocolate éclair

Forget-me-knot

The man who would forget a lot had just walked out his door.
He'd stopped and started wondering what on earth he'd come out for.
He couldn't for the life of him recall the reason why,
And so, he went inside again and drew a heavy sigh.
While trying to remember his original intention,
He drifted onto other things that barely rate a mention,
Then got the smallest inkling that a letter was involved,
But drifted off again before the matter was resolved.
It's true there was a letter which was why he'd ventured out,
A letter with a course that one could say was roundabout,
The same man who was address*er* was also address*ee*,
It said, "REMIND ME TO REMEMBER HOW FORGETFUL I CAN BE!"

Periodic Mabel

Be careful when her iron's low,
She gets a bit unstable,
Her glare, it gets a neon glow -
That's Periodic Mabel.

Mercurial and furrow-browed,
Your logic she'll disable.
No silver lining has the cloud
Of Periodic Mabel.

Like any vial of arsenic,
She needs a warning label.
Her mood's as good as gold then, flick!
It's Periodic Mabel.

She'll hardly pause for oxygen
While ranting on a table.
Get out of there with speed akin
To fibre optic cable.
Your mettle would be beaten thin
By Periodic Mabel.

We're led toward no moral though

Unlike a children's fable.
No elementary truth could flow
From Periodic Mabel.

Greta

There once was a servant called Greta
Whose life really could've been better
So, she went overseas
And found artisan cheese
Now she makes an award-winning feta

Derek

There once was a weatherman, Derek
Whose interests were all atmospheric
He loved sun, rain or snow
And the winds that would blow
As for clouds, they were downright mesmeric

Malcolm

There once was a baby called Malcolm
Whose rashes were eased by some talcum
With no pain round the bum
He smiled at his mum
And she smiled back and whispered, "You're welcome."

The Cricketers' Cry

How's that!?
How was that one!?
Point your index finger at the sun!
He has never made his ground
And there's high fives all around.
It was crazy to attempt a second run.

How's that!?
How was that one!?
You can't allow injustice to be done!
We all heard it but the ump.
Now the bowler's got the hump
And the batsman will go on and get a ton.

How's that!?
How was that one!?
There's no way that his arm ball would've spun!
It was missing off and leg
And likely hitting middle peg.
We aren't standing here appealing just for fun.

How's that?
How was that won?

Some long deliberations have begun.
Be it underarm or underhanded,
Tampering or roughly sanded,
Gentlemanly conduct's come undone.

Susie
There once was a party girl, Susie
Whose life was ongoingly boozy
So she went to rehab
Which was utterly drab
Since the place had no bar or jacuzzi

Rory
There once was a fisherman called Rory
Who landed a record John Dory
But tragically he
Got tipped in the sea
By his shipmate who claimed all the glory

Noah
There once was a farmer called Noah
Who favoured the ride-upon mower
But he mowed at high speed
And caused a stampede
Now he drives it around a lot slower

<u>Julia</u>

I know a girl named Julia
Who's really quite peculiar.
She is, perhaps, a beauty of unparalleled extreme,
But this is rather tempered by a lowly self-esteem.
Where I might see perfection,
She looks at her reflection
And wants for some correction
On a section of herself.
I find it so disquieting,
Her senses must be rioting
And all the books on dieting she has upon her shelf
Are testament and tantamount to scant amount of reason.
Should Julia care to prosecute, she'd charge herself with treason
"Now, Julia," say I,
"You'll waste away and die
If persist you will with fast and pill
Till taken ill and why?"
For where is beauty Julia

But in beholder's eye.
And though you may behold yourself
That mirror tells a lie.
My Julia, you're truly a most wonderful young
girl.
Your shapely guise, your thighs, your eyes,
your hair's exquisite curl,
Your lips, your hips, your fingertips, are
equally sublime,
Obsession led digression then, is more than just
a crime.
Please look at where it takes you to
And look at what it makes you do
And realise, while you're looking, who
Is paying a price respecting few
Of life's essential rules.
As stubborn as a thousand mules,
Miss Julia, with death she duels
And lacking efficacious tools
Means I shall pray with other fools
That one day she'll see sense.
Then gastronomic recompense,
Resultant happy consequence
And healthy from that moment hence
Our Julia would prosper.

<u>Dunbreathen Cemetery</u>

There was a man who died
After jumping in the Clyde.
He knew he couldn't swim
But he did it on a whim.

And a granny who was cherished
Has unfortunately perished.
While half-way through a scone
She was there, then she was gone.

A tourist is now deceased
Since the scooter that he leased
Had its brakes completely fail
Near a cliff, along a trail.

And a gentleman expired
On the day that he retired.
It was terribly bad luck
When the bolt of lightning struck.

It was curtains for a teacher
When she stood upon a creature
That was poisonous and small
Which she didn't see at all.

And a pair of local crazies
Are now pushing up the daisies
After leaping from a height
In a brave attempt at flight.

While he seemed to be robust,
Alas, a farmer bit the dust.
And his cows just milled around
As he lay there on the ground.

And a lady of great size
Has met with her demise
For there's only so much cake
That the human heart can take.

A man who loved French toast
Has given up the ghost
This major fan of eggy bread
Died peacefully in bed

And a businessman has croaked,
They assumed, because he smoked
But it wasn't nicotine
It was rupturing his spleen.

The guy who didn't duck it

Has quite sadly kicked the bucket.
He was crewing on a yacht
But the boom, he saw it not.

And a clown has passed away
After turning very grey.
No-one noticed for a while
Through his make-up and his smile.

A man is six foot under
After quite a silly blunder.
He neglected to look right
When he crossed the road one night.

And a man has met his maker,
A devoted picture-taker
Who was photographing trees
And disturbed a hive of bees.

All these poor departed souls
Had their passions and their goals,
But their time arrived to die -
Now Dunbreathen's where they lie.

Ham Let Loose

Tubby or not tubby: fat is the question.
Whether 'tis nobler that I dine to suffer
The slings and arrows of outrageous portions
Or forsake qualms against these leafy nibbles.
And by disposing of them, to sigh, to weep
No more. Give frier deep away we end
The heartburn and a thousand artery blocks
That flesh is heir to. 'Twas a consumption
Stoutly to be dished. To sigh – to weep
To weep, perchance to scheme – ay, there's the grub.
For in that weepy mess what schemes may come,
When we have truffle quaffed that haughty oil.
Such grievous flaws – there's the neglect
That makes our gluttony of no long life.
For who would share the whipped cream scones of jam.
The ingestion's long – the bowed man's consuming.
The pangs for these pies are love, the slaw's delay.
The insolence of scoffage, and the sponge.
That pastry's merit and the unworthy cake,

When he himself might quietly bake.
With bare bod, who would cuddles bear?
To grunt and sweat under a leery wife,
But that the dread of humping's faster breath.
The unbeloved quandary 'pon who's torn.
No shoveler discerns, guzzles the swill
And makes us rather fear the ills we have,
And lie to others that we knew not of.
Thus, chocolate does make cowards of us all
And thus the lentil stew of absolution
Is sicklied over with the scales' fast retort,
And exercises of great stitch and movement.
With this we turn the currant buns away
And chose the game of action.

Gus

There once was a driver called Gus
Whose job involved driving a bus
Though his wife liked to say,
"Honey, how was your day?"
There was never that much to discuss

<u>The Life of the Party</u>

I wish I were the life of the party
But fear it's something I could never be,
For I really don't enjoy it in the slightest
When everyone's attention is on me.

I cannot be outrageous or insightful.
I cannot sing or tell amusing jokes.
My anecdotes are far from being delightful.
I'm someone others always have to coax.

My conversation draws no eager crowd.
My confidence too fleetingly survives.
Not all my thoughts should manifest aloud.
My ready wit belatedly arrives.

Alas, I am resigned to being the fellow,
Begrudgingly attending each soiree,
Blending in superbly with the background
And hoping that's exactly where I stay.

<u>Cadence Willoughby-Jeffries</u>

Mr Cadence Willoughby-Jeffries lives alone.
You'd be asked to leave your message at the tone
If you ever rang him on the phone.
For it's very rare this fellow is at home
Unlike his one and only garden gnome.
Mr Cadence Willoughby-Jeffries likes to roam
Along winding roads and fields of green,
Up rolling hills, through small ravine,
He'll wander through a painted scene
Or past a sculptured figurine.
The places that he hasn't been
Are very few and far between.
A day so warm, the air so clean,
The distant setting sun would mean
Another day was done.
He'd had his fill of roaming fun.

Accepting as he always did, the situation thus,
He walked along the road awhile and waited for a bus.
On arrival at his residence, he entered through the door

And tripped and nearly fell as he'd done many
times before.
The same old piece of carpet he'd elected to
ignore
Had once again reminded him of all that
needed doing,
Repairing or adjusting, discarding or renewing.
Mr Cadence Willoughby-Jeffries was impatient
with such things.
He saw them as intrusion on the world to
which he clings.
They scared away his freedoms – blunt his very
being,
Arrest him from the romance he insisted upon
seeing.
He'll sit a while and close his eyes, exhausted
by the day,
Then gaze outside his window at the many led
astray.

Mr. Cadence Willoughby-Jeffries don't desire
their consent,
You need no validation from the spiritually
spent.
Forget about the masses and their ludicrous
ideals,

Who shudder when they witness someone doing as he feels.
The individual frowned upon is often very brave
And secretly admired by the many who behave.
So, let then have their micro greens, their Venezuelan coffee beans,
Their multiple mesmeric screens and ventilated skinny jeans.

Jonah
There once was a traveller called Jonah
Who ran with the bulls in Pamplona
But it didn't go well
When he tripped and he fell
Now he urgently needs a blood donor

Neil
There was a psychologist called Neil
Who would ask, "How did that make you feel?"
And when patients replied
He was laughing inside
But pretending he cared a great deal

Dispositional Concourse

Happiness arrived with a smile on his face.
Fear was trembling, crouched behind a wall.
Mystery appeared then disappeared without a trace.
Distrusting wasn't having it at all.

Anger was demanding that he not be pushed around.
Confidence strode confidently in.
Timid tried so hard to hide and not to make a sound.
Impatience was most eager to begin.

Bigoted spoke up because he had to have his say.
Uncertainty could not make up his mind.
Boredom and indifference were not bothered either way.
Apathy was already resigned.

Curious inspected what was happening from afar.
Famous was the centre of attention.

Sickly turned up pallid with his gall stones in a jar.
Bewildered wasn't at the right convention.

Gregarious was mingling in a very shallow way.
Abusive swore with middle finger raised.
Gullible was sitting there being nicely led astray.
Nonchalance was sitting there unfazed.

Persuasive had convinced the host to let him through the door.
Pedantic straightened pictures on the wall.
Demented took off all his clothes and lay down on the floor.
Aesthetic saw the beauty in it all.

Anxiety was worried that his anxiousness would show.
Contented was quite happy with his lot.
Depressed was unimpressed at best and wallowing in woe.
Forgetful wasn't there as he forgot.

Imperious was organizing people into teams.

Paranoia's ears began to burn.
Romantic offered flowers to the woman of his dreams.
Poetic penned a poem on his return.

Tara
There was a survivor called Tara
Whose plane had crashed near the Sahara
There was many a threat
And the heat made her sweat
But much worse was her runny mascara

Mitch
There once was a plumber called Mitch
Who, while busily digging a ditch
Found a coin made of gold
Seven hundred years old
And said, "I'll be a son-of-a-bitch!"

Joan
There was an investor called Joan
Who secured a sizeable loan
But she got very slack
In paying it back
And her whereabouts now are unknown

<u>**Avian Air**</u>

It's a curious thing -
What would make a bird sing?
Is it just that it can?
Or some much greater plan?
Are they happy in song?
Do they ever go wrong?
Like a note out of tune
On a cold afternoon
(Something I've never heard
At least not from a bird).
Do they practice somewhere?
I expect that it's rare
To be witness to this type of scene –
Where our fine feathered friend
Would spend hours on end
Perfecting the notes
And the spaces between.
But then maybe it's best
If such mysteries remain
For in solving them
Surely, we've little to gain.
One could speculate, theorise,
Wonder or guess,
But in doing so

One might appreciate less,
This phenomenon nature presents every day,
These melodious songs that come drifting our
way.

Claude
There once was an architect, Claude
Whose designs were at times rather flawed
With the client bemused
And the builder confused
He'd go back to the old drawing board

Sophie
There once was a baker called Sophie
Whose life was exceedingly loafy
But she made the best bread
That you'd ever be fed
And for this she was given a trophy

The Course of True Love

Oh, Helen Watermelon,
I did love you very much.
I thought about you constantly
And so longed for your touch.

And Molly Cauliflower, too,
My love for you was real.
The depths to which my passions went,
I barely could conceal.

But both these girls rejected me,
They shot me down in flames.
'Tis I, the tender innocent
That such rejection shames.

So, this is where I find myself,
Upstanding on a ledge
And leaping to my death for girls
Whose names are fruit and veg…

Alas, the ledge was not that high,
I've only sprained my knee,
But as I lie in hospital
Who's this approaching me…?

A pair of gorgeous nurses
Attending at my bed.
Seems fate chose not to end my life
But lead me here instead…

"I'd like to introduce myself
I'm very glad we've met
My name is Aubrey Strawberry
You'll have lovely names I bet…"

The nurses looked at Aubrey,
One was blonde and one brunette.
They said, "I'm Janet Pomegranate."
"And I'm Bernadette Courgette."

Well, Aubrey being Aubrey
Was enamoured even more,
But really very ill-prepared
For what they had in store…

"Oh, Aubrey we are sorry
But you're not our type of guy.
We know another nurse though
Who just might be worth a try."

"She's pretty as a picture

And as cute as any panda.
We think you'll like her name too…
It's Amanda Coriander."

Greg

There once was a skier called Greg
Who fell badly and fractured his leg
As he lay on the slope
Having given up hope
A Saint Bernard turned up with a keg

Lizzie

There once was a doctor called Lizzie
Who always was frantically busy
And the stress of a day
Saw her hair turning grey
And from pleasantly straight to quite frizzy

Christine

There once was a cleaner called Cristine
Employed in a chapel called Sistine
And she worked until spent
Every hour God sent
Bent on keeping the place looking pristine

Verity versus Sincerity

Verity suffered from vanity
And bursts of alarming profanity
Which peppered a graceless inanity,
All embraced by a dismal mundanity.
There were questions regarding her sanity
And rumours of gross inhumanity.

So, they made a reality show
About Verity's life on the go
And it took many takes in a row
To help the reality flow.
Though the ratings began pretty low,
Soon they rapidly started to grow.

Because Verity's life was so real,
The show had enormous appeal.
We saw Verity midst an ordeal
And then Verity trying to heal.
We saw Verity giggle and squeal
And then Verity showing her steel.

We saw Verity starting a craze
And then millions who copied her ways.
We heard so many splendid clichés

From the millions who offered her praise.
We saw Verity catching some rays
As she peered through reality's haze.

And the audience grew and it grew.
She was only despised by a few -
Disinclined to forsake their IQ,
But their voices would never get through.
They were drowned by a clamouring zoo
And their worship of that which was true.

At last, Verity's worlds would collide
In a way that could not be denied.
She had no moral compass to guide.
She had no hope of turning the tide.
No assistance from those alongside,
Prudence just came along for the ride,
As for Charity, she was implied.
There was nothing and nowhere to hide
As the soul reached the end of its slide.
All its love and vitality dried,
Every donut was baked and not fried…
And a civilisation had died.

Daphne McKnatt and her Fat Tartan Cat

Old Daphne McKnatt and her fat tartan cat
Lived in a one-bedroom Aberdeen flat.

One day a girl with her hair in a plait
Knocked on the door of their Aberdeen flat.
She'd only come round for some tea and a chat,
But the door opened up, the cat hissed and spat
And Daphne McKnatt said, "Piss off you brat!"
So away ran the girl with her hair in a plait.

One day a man in a paisley cravat
Knocked on the door of their Aberdeen flat.
Soon he was wishing he hadn't done that -
The door opened up, the cat hissed and spat
And Daphne McKnatt said, "Piss off you twat!"
So away ran the man in a paisley cravat.

One day a boy with a ball and a bat
Knocked on the door of their Aberdeen flat.
It was not the address he was supposed to be at.
The door opened up, the cat hissed and spat
And Daphne McKnatt said, "Piss off you brat!"
So away ran the boy with the ball and the bat.

One day a man in a bright vest and hat
Knocked on the door of their Aberdeen flat.
He was there to repair the McKnatt thermostat
But before he could wipe his two feet on the
mat,
The door opened up, the cat hissed and spat
And Daphne McKnatt said, "Piss off you twat!"
So away ran the man in a bright vest and hat.

Old Daphne McKnatt and her fat tartan cat
Both froze to death in their Aberdeen flat.
The cause of their deaths was indeed
thermostatic,
If only they'd learned to be more diplomatic.

Shaun

There once was a driver called Shaun
Who would lean a bit hard on his horn
Then somebody snapped
Broke his window and slapped
Till he wished that he'd never been born

<u>The Mad King</u>

Gwendoline, my dear,
Would you please come over here?
I've something you might like to see.
'Twas something Edward gave to me,
A priceless object few could own,
My dear, it's called an ice-cream cone.
Its value lies in scarcity,
Said Edward, "There are only three."
But what of art and artistry?
They've never meant that much to me.
All I see is form and tone
And beauty in my ice-cream cone.

Now, Gwendoline I must protest,
The lengthy sleeves upon this vest.
These men in coats of grimy white,
Advising me on what is right.
They dare unseat me from my throne.
They've come to take my ice-cream cone.
But no, their interest seems to be
In wanting to take care of me.
My friends, I don't require care,
Your presence is not needed here.
Why can't you leave a king alone

To contemplate his ice-cream cone?

Beth

There was an old lady called Beth
Who lisped when she spoke about death
So when a relation
Proposed a cremation
She thought for a bit then said, "Yeth."

Allan

There once was a drunkard called Allan
Who used to drink rum by the gallon
But one evening in May
After drinking all day
He fell backwards and busted his melon

Guy

There once was a writer called Guy
Who wrote novels that no-one would buy
Then a story he wrote
Seemed to hit the right note
And he still doesn't really know why

The Lonely Scotsman

Ah'm Jimmy wi' a jester's hat,
The bells gae tinkle tankle.
Ah'm jumpin' roond an' daein' flips
An' bustin' up mah ankle.

Ah'm limpin' wi' a walkin' stick
And wavin' it aboot,
Then starin' like an owlie bird
What disnae give a hoot.

Ah'll haver at the baker's girl,
She's skin that seems tae glow.
Ah'd tell her that I love her
But her eyes already know.

Ah'm arf tae work in safety boots
An' trudgin' doon mah street,
Then toilin' wi' a bastard lot
Who've givin' up complete.

But there's nae a breath o' wind aboot
Tae blow away yer cares
And nae a ray of sun come oot
Tae warm away yer fears.

There's nae a crashin' wave nearby
Tae drown oot all yer thinkin'
And no way t' suppress the bad
Nae drugs, nae sex, nae drinkin'.

Grant

There once was a hooligan called Grant
Who made up his own racist chant
But was easy to catch
Since he went to each match
And his IQ was that of a plant

Wendy

There once was a gymnast called Wendy
Whose body was freakishly bendy
She could easily compose
With only her toes
A hairdo that looked rather trendy

Sam

There once was an actor called Sam
Whose life was a bit of a sham
For he'd constantly claim
An unparalleled fame
But had once done an ad for some jam

Reality Adaption Technician

His ability to lie was most impressive from the start.
From very early on he realised lying was an art.
A falsely painted picture for the audience before him.
The truth became an option that would only serve to bore him.
His parents were enthused about this talent that he showed,
"A journalist, an actor or a barrister!" they glowed.

It began when caught red-handed doing something he should not.
He knew he was in bother, rather more than just a spot.
He did his best not-guilty face but things were looking bleak.
The constable sarcastically encouraged him to speak,
"Please go ahead young man and I shall take this lying down."
His right hand poised at notebook with a concentrated frown.

But then was spun a tale somewhat joyous to behold.
The constable took every word as genuine as gold.
A desperate situation solved and done so with some style.
He walked away a blameless man attempting not to smile,
With power coursing through his veins, the power to deceive
And the ease with which he'd done it he could scarcely believe.

So, what a tangled web was woven from that moment hence,
Up until one fateful day when finally he saw sense.
It first appeared quite vaguely in a dreamlike fuzzy way.
A long-forgotten concept from a long-forgotten day,
Then the painful realisation of the havoc he had wreaked.
His falsehood, fabrication and dishonesty had peaked.

"What can I do, my point of view has thoroughly reversed.
To those whom I have wronged, they will be fully reimbursed.
I'll mend my ways, I'll spend my days providing them support,
And throw myself sincerely on the mercy of this court."
Though someone in the gallery was heard to loudly scoff,
The rest were sympathetic and the judge just let him off.

Tom

There once was a soldier called Tom
Who was tasked with defusing a bomb
But his colourblind eyes
Caused a scattered demise
Which did greatly disturb his aplomb

<u>Ambition Attrition</u>

I used to want to change the world.
Now, I just want to change the channel.

I used to want to save the whales.
Now, I just want to save a document.

I used to want to find myself.
Now, I just want to find my glasses.

I used to want to make my fortune.
Now, I just want to make do.

I used to want to climb Everest.
Now, I just want to climb into bed.

I used to want to fall in love.
Now, I just want to fall asleep.

I used to want to leave my mark.
Now, I just want to leave.

The End

Guide to "Watson a Name"

Feel exhausted, And he's off
A neater finish, Owing money
Page turner, Fake leg
Crisp lettuce and stewed apple, Nearly had him
Chaotic, Evening all and police dog
Human error, Jaw dropping
Bench warmer, Bone idle
Herbivore, Stand up all day
Proof reading, Build your own
Car alarm, It's all better now
Barbed wire and Barricade, Huge honour
You and who's army, It's on your head
Roof is leaking, Marrying couples
Antiques, Suit of armour
True delight, Free delivery
An enormous profit, Evict a tenant
Dug deep, Petrified
Beneficial, Responsible
Law abiding, Nick my car
Just in case he falls, Loose wire
Raw emotion, Head in her hands
A mosquito, I'm a looney